MARTÍN DE LEÓN

TEJANO EMPRESARIO

Martín de León

Tejano Empresario

Judy Alter

Illustrated by Patrick Messersmith

State ✦ House
Press

McMurry University
Abilene, Texas

Library of Congress Cataloging-in-Publication Data

Alter, Judy, 1938-
    Martín de León : Tejano empresario / Judy Alter ; illustrated by Patrick Messersmith.
      p. cm.–(The stars of Texas series)
    Includes bibliographical references and index.
    ISBN-13: 978-1-933337-08-1 (hardcover: alk. paper)
    ISBN-10: 1-933337-08-7 (hardcover: alk. paper) 1. Victoria
(Tex.)–History–Juvenile literature. 2. León, Martín de, 1765-1833–Juvenile literature.
3. Mexican Americans–Texas–Victoria–Biography–Juvenile literature.
4. Pioneers–Texas–Victoria–Biography–Juvenile literature. 5. Texas–Biography–Juvenile
literature. I. Messersmith, Patrick. II. Title.

F394.V6A45 2006
976.4'125–dc22

2006033214

State House Press
McMurry Station, Box 637
Abilene, TX 79697-0637
(325) 572-3974
www.mcwhiney.org/press

Distributed by Texas A&M University Press Consortium
(800) 826-8911
www.tamu.edu/upress

Printed in the United States of America

ISBN-13: 978-1-933337-08-1
ISBN-10: 1-933337-08-7

Book designed by Rosenbohm Graphic Design

THE STARS OF TEXAS SERIES

Other books in this series include:

Henrietta King: Rancher and Philanthropist

Mirabeau B. Lamar: Second President of Texas

Miriam "Ma" Ferguson: First Woman Governor of Texas

Free workbooks available on-line at
www.mcwhiney.org/press

Contents

Chapter 1

INTRODUCTION

✳✳✳✳✳

In the 1820s Texas was part of the province of Coahuila y Tejas. Like all of present-day Mexico, the land then called Tejas was under the control of Spain. A governor in San Antonio presided over Tejas in the name of the Spanish king.

Not many people lived in Tejas. Spain considered it a wild land, too far from the civilized cities of New Spain (Mexico), and the Spanish government had no money to encourage settlement of the region. Spain wanted to settle Tejas and gain money from land grants. The Spanish government finally granted land rights to a few Anglo men from the United States. These men, known as empresarios, petitioned for grants of large tracts of land and then acted as land agents or contractors, bringing Anglo settlers to live on their land. When a settler bought land from Mexico, the empresario received a commission, usually in more land, which he in turn could sell.

Most, but not all, empresarios were Anglos from the United States. Moses Austin of Missouri was probably the first empresario to start a colony in Texas, and Austin's Colony is the best known. Moses' son, Stephen F. Austin, became the most famous empresario and a leader in the government of the new Republic of Texas in the 1830s. Sterling Robertson was another important empresario. Robertson's Colony and Austin's Colony were both in Central Texas. Other empresarios were Green DeWitt, Samuel May Williams, James Power, James Hewetson, John McMullen, James McGloin, and Arthur G. Wavell.

Martín de León was the only Tejano or Mexican empresario to settle a colony in Texas. He established his colony in southeast Texas,

"Tejas" is the Spanish word for Texas. Before its independence, Texas was part of the Spanish (and then Mexican) province of Coahuila y Tejas.

near the Gulf Coast, and brought settlers there from Mexico. His was the only completely successful colony in Texas besides Austin's. De León founded the city of Victoria, Texas, and had several ranches in the area. The largest was the Santa Margarita, his home ranch.

Don Martín was a tall man, over six feet in height, with a fair complexion. He was known for his courage, his good horsemanship, and his skill as a brave Indian fighter. He began fighting Indians as a young man in the Mexican province of Nuevo Santander (now Tamaulipas), and he found himself still fighting Indians at his colony in Tejas. Don Martín de León governed and defended his colony with the help of his four sons.

In 1833, a cholera epidemic came west from New Orleans and swept through Tejas. Don Martín was the first victim to die in his colony. He had been about to build a huge cathedral in Victoria. If he had lived, Victoria might have had a cathedral as beautiful as the greatest cathedrals Spain.

Before he died, de León had actively supported the cause of more independence for Tejas and the creation of a separate Mexican province from Coahuila. His sons continued to fight for new rights for Texians and Tejanos, giving money and goods to the Texas Volunteers. But after the fall of the Alamo and the massacre at Goliad, Texians disliked and distrusted anyone of Mexican descent. Many thought all Mexicans should return to Mexico. The de León family suffered from this prejudice and lost their land and livestock. Without a way to support themselves, they left Texas, lived briefly in Louisiana, and finally returned to Mexico.

"Texian" is the term for an Anglo resident of Tejas which was used until the 1850s.

"Tejano" is the term used for a Texas resident of Spanish decent.

In 1972, the State of Texas recognized the great unfairness of the treatment of the de León family. Texas state historical markers were placed at the family graves in the Evergreen Cemetery in Victoria. Patricia de León, great-granddaughter of the empresario, attended the ceremony, along with Dr. Ricardo Victoria of Mexico, the great-grandson of Mexican President Guadalupe Victoria, for whom Don Martín named the city of Victoria.

The story of Don Martín de León and his family is an important part of Texas history, not only for the story of one family but also for the story of Mexicans in Texas.

Chapter 2

A Privileged Childhood and Settlement in Tejas

✳✳✳✳✳

Martín de León was born in the town of Burgos, in the Mexican province of Nuevo Santander, a province which sat on the Gulf Coast. A portion of Nuevo Santander extended into the province of Coahuila y Tejas. The viceroy, representative of the King of Spain in Mexico, encouraged settlement of the area. Martín's parents moved to Nuevo Santander for the adventure and opportunity, just as their son would seek the same things in Tejas. Martín was descended from wealthy Spanish nobles who had been educated in European cities and knew European kings and queens. In Spain, they had been explorers, statesmen, and military men. They had lived in

A jacal is a house or fence made of thin sticks driven into the ground and plastered over with mud. Jacals were common on the frontier.

the Spanish city of Burgos, known for its beautiful architecture and its cathedrals, many of which were built in the twelfth century. The de Leóns came to Mexico in 1650, and Martín's parents named the town where they settled Burgos, after their home in Spain.

✳✳✳

The Adventures of a Young Man

Young Martín was given the best education possible and did well in school. His father wanted him to continue his education in Europe, but Martín was not interested in more education. He wanted to go into business for himself, though he chose an unusual way to do so. He became a muleteer, commanding a train of pack mules, and traveled to the mountains in northern Nuevo Santander. He was a *mayordomo*, or head muleteer, and

Mustangs were descendants of pure-bred Spanish horses that had strayed from their Spanish masters. They lived free on the prairie, without human contact.

he hired other men to help him. He may have worked for a mine, carrying ore, or for the government, carrying tobacco to authorized stores (legally, tobacco could only be sold in stores authorized by the Spanish government). He might also have traded local goods for merchandise he brought from cities to the south. He would have then sold the local goods at a profit when he returned south.

In 1790, at the age of twenty, Martín joined the Fieles de Burgos militia regiment to fight Indians that were attacking settlers in his province. Spanish officers were in charge of the regiment. Martín was a good soldier and moved up in rank quickly. After only five years, he was appointed a captain of the regiment. He reached the highest rank that a man born in Mexico could reach. Even

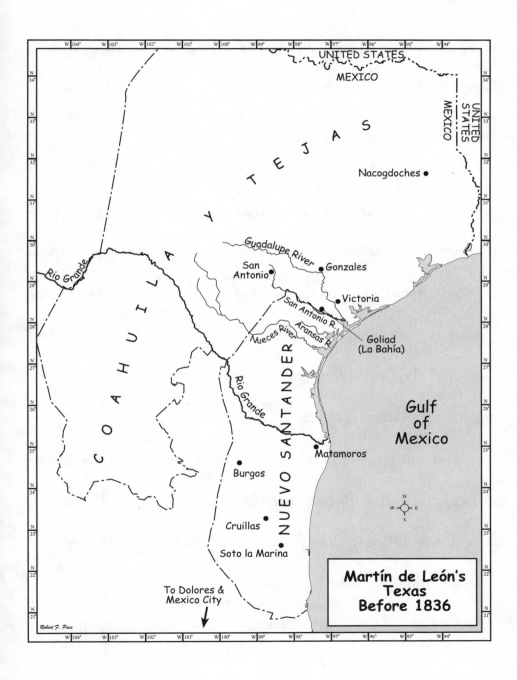

UNITED STATES
MEXICO

MEXICO
UNITED STATES

T E J A S

Nacogdoches

C O A H U I L A   Y

Rio Grande

Guadalupe River

San Antonio

Gonzales

Victoria

San Antonio R.

Aransas R.

Goliad
(La Bahía)

Nueces River

N U E V O   S A N T A N D E R

Rio Grande

Gulf
of
Mexico

Matamoros

Burgos

Cruillas

Soto la Marina

To Dolores &
Mexico City

**Martín de León's
Texas
Before 1836**

Robert J. Pace

though he considered his family as good as any born in Spain, Spanish officials considered those born in Mexico as second-class citizens.

✳✳✳

Marriage and a Family

In 1795, Martín married Patricia de la Garza, the daughter of his commander. She was born in Soto la Marina in Nuevo Santander in 1775. Not much is known of her family, except that she brought a large dowry to the marriage, a sign that her family was well to do. Her father gave her twelve mares, four two-year-old colts, five tame horses, five untamed horses, several donkeys and cows.

Like her husband, Patricia liked the outdoors and the adventure of pioneering. Both Martín and Patricia were attracted to ranch life, and they settled in the town of Cruillas in Nuevo Santander and began ranching. Their first child, Fernando, was born in Cruillas in 1798. A second child, Maria Candelaria was born in 1800. The other children of the family were all born in Tejas: Silvestre (1802); Maria Guadalupe "Lupita" (1804); Felix (1806); Agapito (1808); Maria de Jesús "Chucha" (1810); Refugia (1812); Augustina (1814); and Francisca (1818).

In 1801, Martín traveled to Tejas for the first time, riding with his regiment on the road between San Antonio and Nacogdoches in search of a filibuster named Philip Nolan. Nolan was suspected of leading an unauthorized expedition into Mexico. De León found a beautiful land with wildflowers growing in the middle of the tall grasses on the prairies. Some of the grass grew four to six feet in height, and there were numerous rivers and streams. Large herds of deer, buffalo, and antelope roamed the prairies, along with herds of wild mustangs. Martín visited La Bahía, Nacogdoches, and San Antonio.

A filibuster is a soldier of fortune or an adventurer that engages in military action in a foreign country for personal gain.

***

THE MOVE TO TEJAS

Martín de León knew he wanted to live on this beautiful land. He traveled back to Mexico to get his wife and children, their servants, and their household goods. Together he and his wife invested her dowry in this move to Tejas. They loaded carts with provisions so that they could travel from place to place before choosing the land where they wanted to live. They settled first in a community on the San Antonio River. Unlike Anglo-American settlers, who tended to build their dwellings apart from one another, Tejanos usually settled in family groups.

Martín had brought cattle, horses, mules, and goats from Mexico. He began rounding up mustangs to tame and enclosed a pasture to hold them. He began to build a casa grande or big house to keep his family safe from Indian raids. It was probably a series of rooms, each with its own fireplace, built around a courtyard. The number of rooms a man built depended on his wealth. The rooms usually had no windows but did have gun slits, and a wall outside the house provided a barricade.

Patricia was the patrona of the ranch. She supervised the other women in preparing food for the main house. She taught her own daughters to embroider bedspreads, altar clothes, and upholstery furniture. They wove wool into blankets and made toilet soap from tallow. Once a week, the women did the washing—and every day they took a siesta. This routine was broken twice a year by the roundup and occasionally by trips to San Antonio, especially at Christmas time.

Martín petitioned the Spanish government to allow him to buy his land. Since 1800, Mexico had been trying to free itself from Spain. Because Martín was not loyal to Spain and supported those who fought to rid Mexico of Spanish rule, he was in disfavor with the Spanish authorities in Mexico. His petition was rejected.

Martín moved his ranching operation to the Nueces River, near present-day San Patricio. He called the ranch Santa Margarita. In 1809, he petitioned the government again. Again, he was refused.

In 1812, word came of violent unrest among of the poor in Mexico against the rich, uprisings that included the slaughter of entire families. Martín did not worry until the revolutionaries were rumored to be headed toward San Antonio and La Bahía. He packed up his family and servants and returned to Patricia's hometown of Soto la Marina, located in a part of Mexico safe from the uprisings. By September, the government had established its power again, and it was safe for the de León family to return to the Santa Margarita. They found it badly damaged. They decided not to rebuild and instead moved their belongings to land on the Aransas River, closer to La Bahía. By now, Martín's sons were old enough to help him build the *casa grande* for the family and jacales for the servants and their families.

Chapter 3

THE DE LEÓN COLONY

✳✳✳✳✳

In September 1810 Miguel Hidalgo y Costilla, a Mexican

priest in the small town of Dolores in the province of Guanajuato,

ordered the arrest of all Spaniards in the area. Then he issued a cry

for Mexicans to rise up against the Spanish. His plea became known

as "El Grito de Dolores" ("the Cry of Dolores"). Today Mexico cele-

brates its independence on September 16 because of Father Hidalgo's

rebellion.

Father Hidalgo's uprising had an unexpected result. Spanish

troops were withdrawn from presidios in Tejas because the soldiers

were needed to control the uprisings in Mexico that began with "El

Grito." Settlers in Tejas were left without protection. Lipan Apache and Comanche Indians began to steal from them, and some settlers were massacred. Martín worried about his family. Since no other families lived near his compound, the de Leóns could not band together with others for protection. In 1816, he moved his wife and children to San Antonio for safety. In San Antonio, he supported those who believed in government by the citizens rather than the Spanish government ruled by a royal family. When he considered it safe again, his family joined him at the ranch.

In 1821, Mexico finally won its independence from Spain. By then Martín had five or six thousand head of cattle, along with horses and mules. In 1823, he drove his first herd of cattle east to the markets in New Orleans, making him one of the first trail drivers in Tejas. After that, he regularly sold his livestock in markets at New Orleans, and he made a great deal of money. His custom was to buy supplies for his family and the workers on his ranch in New Orleans.

Father Hidalgo's "Grito de Dolores" began Mexico's long struggle for independence from Spain. The first rebels were mostly native Indians and mestizos (people of mixed race). They fought with clubs, slings, axes, knives, and machetes. The rebellion was very bloody. Many criollos (Mexican-born Spaniards) did not support this violence.

He was by all measures a successful man, but he still wanted to own his land. That had been denied him earlier by the Spanish government, but Martín was in favor with the new Mexican government because he had supported independence from Spain.

One year when he drove a large herd of livestock to New Orleans and bought supplies to take back to his ranch, the only ship he could find to take the supplies to Tejas was a pirate ship that belonged to a Frenchman named Ramon La Fou. De León chartered the ship to deliver supplies to his ranch. In return, La Fou wanted an official pardon from the Mexican government for his activities as a pirate. De León promised to help get that pardon.

The boat sailed for the mouth of the Rio Grande River at Matamoras. Martín went ashore to secure the pardon. He left his son, Felix, on the boat as proof of his good intentions. General Don Felix de la Garza, the commanding officer at Tamaulipas and a friend of Martín's, granted the pardon. Martín decided it was a good time to ask again for a charter to act as an empresario. He petitioned the government in Mexico City, and this time his petition was granted. By then the empresario system was established, and Martín feared that Stephen F. Austin was filling all the available land with Anglos.

✳✳✳

BUILDING A SETTLEMENT

Martín traveled throughout Nuevo Santander recruiting settlers, but he had a hard time finding families willing to move to Tejas. When he had enough settlers, he appeared before the provincial deputy in San Antonio with his petition requesting permission to found a colony on the Guadalupe River. He promised to bring forty-one families at his own expense and to establish a town. Patricia had recently received an inheritance of almost $10,000 as well as cattle, horses, and mules. They used the money to establish their colony on the Guadalupe River.

As an empresario, Martín could now assume the title of Don. It was a term of respect for male leaders. In 1824 he established the city of Nuestra Señora de Guadalupe de Jesús Victoria (today known as Victoria). He named it for the first president of Mexico, Don Guadalupe Victoria. At first the city shared a council with the town of Goliad. Martín petitioned to separate the two cities but that was denied because a land commissioner had not yet been sent to grant titles to the colonists. De León was permitted to have a representative on the Goliad council or *ayuntamiento*, and a land commissioner for Victoria was appointed. Don Martín established St. Mary's Catholic Church in the new community, with Father Eubaldy Estany as the first pastor. Today it is the second oldest Catholic parish in Texas.

Don Martín's sons helped him lay out the town. They assisted the settlers in finding the land they wanted. Setting up a town was much more complicated than establishing a ranch. There was a church square and a market square to plan and town lots to assign, the best locations going to members of Don Martín's family.

Don Martín and Patricia were no longer young adventurers. He was sixty years old, and his wife was nearing fifty. Their first house, which had a dirt floor, was located on the present site of St. Mary's Church and Nazareth Convent in the city of Victoria. Later Don Martín built a log house on the Garcitas Creek of the Guadalupe River, nine miles from town and on one of his

In 1820 the criollos supported Augustín de Iturbide, a military officer, in his leadership to free Mexico from Spain. In 1821, he reached an agreement with Spain whereby that government would turn over control of Mexico but would retrieve the value of its land in good money.

ranches. Legend said the ranch included the land where the French explorer, René Robert Cavalier, Sieur de La Salle, had landed. The family lived alternately on the ranch and in town, depending on cir-cumstances. Similarly, the married children had both ranches and homes in town.

Patricia de León still enjoyed the pioneering life as much as her husband did. On the ranch, they raised corn, beans, and potatoes, and they ate venison, beef, pork, and fish. For greens, they gathered pokeweed and nettles. Homegrown sugar cane was used to make candy and molasses. Doña Patricia also served such traditional Mexican dishes as tortillas and chili con carne.

✳✳✳

DON MARTÍN BECOMES A WEALTHY MAN

The de León children had private tutors and Doña Patricia eventually sent her children to Europe and Mexico to go to school.

But Doña Patricia saw to it that a school was established in the town for the children of colonists, and she and the other women worked tirelessly to teach the colony's children the catechism of the Catholic Church. She believed that religion and education were the responsibilities of the women, and she wanted to bring the traditions of Spain and Mexico to Tejas. The colonists knew that they could turn to Doña Patricia for help when they needed it. She was a full partner in her husband's business ventures and not a silent, obedient wife. Doña Patricia deserves much of the credit for creating a stable community in the colony and, later, in Victoria, and for teaching her daughters to make their own decisions, including business decisions.

As Don Martín's wealth increased, Doña Patricia brought fine furniture and clothes from Europe. The de León home was the most beautiful in the area, and it became a center for social gatherings. Baptisms and weddings were especially important religious and social

Curing Cow Hides

Don Martín's formula for curing cow hides, hand written in his record book dated 1827:

Place a hide in a tub seven feet long, three feet wide; cover it with two feet of water.

Use 90 cups tapomica, 17 cups alum, 12 cups starch, 7 cups salt

Wash well for one week.

Use the same formula again and soak for two weeks.

Use the same formula again, and soak for three weeks. This formula is for thirty hides.

occasions. The parties were almost continuous as six of the ten de León children married and numerous grandchildren were born. Because their family owned a lot of land, the de León children were seen as good matches for the children of neighboring ranchers and other important people. Don Martín was pleased when his daughters married young men with political connections or influence. In that day and time, young women married early. An unmarried woman of twenty-one was practically an old maid. When Fernando, the oldest of the de León children married, the ceremony in the chapel was followed by a feast for the entire town. It took Doña Patricia months to arrange this feast, which lasted for three days. Afterwards, people spoke of the wedding for years.

✳✳✳

Mexico Begins to Pay Attention
to the Colonies

Mexico had no laws that governed the colonies in Tejas. Each empresario made laws for his own colony. In 1824 the Mexican Congress realized that Anglos were moving into Texas in large numbers, and the Congress began to pass laws governing those colonists. Foreigners could not settle near the coast. No empresario could claim more than eleven leagues of land. Immigrants had to swear loyalty to the Catholic Church and promise to be good, moral citizens. Individuals and familiies could only receive land through an empresario. The empresario received extra land for every ten families he settled in Tejas, and colonists would not be taxed for ten years.

Austin's Colony, perhaps because it was the first colony and long established, was not subject to these laws. Probably because the de León Colony was the only one with Mexican settlers, its settlers also were not subject to many of these laws. Settlers in the de León Colony each received one labor of land (177 acres) and a building lot in Victoria.

A conflict over land developed with a neighboring colony. Both de León and empresario Green De Witt claimed the same land. Don Martín was known to own a huge sword, and rumors spread that he would confront De Witt and behead him. De León supposedly went to the De Witt Colony, accompanied by armed men who disarmed De Witt's colonists. The matter was peacefully settled. Don Martín did not use his sword, but the sword is considered an important relic from Victoria's history. The sword was once on display at a school in Victoria and it is said to have once been exhibited at the Alamo, along with the empresario's spurs. Today the location of these relics is not known.

✳✳✳

INDIANS!

Indian attacks were still a great threat to the de León colonists and to others in the area. Because travelers were often robbed and murdered, Don Martín often hid people in his house when Indians were chasing them. After the Indians left, he would help the travelers escape. The Indians called him Captain Vacamucha (many cows). Generally when the Indians came to his home, he raised the white flag of peace. Then he butchered cows and gave them meat. He also gave them whiskey. Once a group of travelers had a cannon lashed to a mule's back. A band of Comanche suddenly appeared. Someone lit the cannon. It fired and scared away the Indians, but it also broke the mule's back.

Another time a band of Karankawa Indians came to Don Martín's ranch. The Indians were painted red, a color that indicated

**To Dye
Cowhides Black**

*(from Don Martín's
record book):
Dissolve extract of dogwood
in water; boil and add blue
stone and a small quantity
of copperas. Add skins
when the liquid is hot. Rub
well, dry, and wash in good
soapsuds. Then wash in
clear water. When nearly
dry, rub all the time or they
will be hard. To dye a hide
purple: leave out the
copperas and blue stone
and add alum.*

they wanted war. Don Martín was home alone with his wife and a few servants. He put a cannon in the doorway and told his wife to be ready to fire it. He stationed servants with rifles at the loopholes on either side of the door. Then he walked out to meet the Indians. They saw the cannon and made the sign for peace. Don Martín gave them beef and blankets.

Don Martín was known to help travelers in many ways besides protecting them from Indians. Once a man came to the ranch and said he needed two horses. He could not pay, but he said he would pay later. When Don Martín agreed to give him the horses, the man was shocked. Don Martín said, "If you do not keep your word, all I have lost is two horses. You will have lost your reputation and self respect."

In 1829, the Mexican government gave Don Martín a contract to bring 150 additional families to his colony. According to the contract, these colonists could settle on land along the Gulf Coast. The contract also allowed Don Martín to take soldiers as colonists, which was not allowed in most colonies.

Chapter 4

TEXAS INDEPENDENCE

✳✳✳✳✳

By the early 1830s, the de León colony was worth a million dollars. Don Martín dreamed of making Victoria a great city, built around a cathedral. When he had visited Burgos, Spain, the home of his ancestors, the cathedrals there inspired him to build an equally beautiful cathedral in Victoria. He sketched the way he wanted the cathedral to look and got estimates for building it. He was ready to bring engineers and architects from Mexico to work on it, when a cholera epidemic hit the colony. Don Martín sent his family to the ranch for their safety, but he remained behind, becoming the first in the colony to die. He was seventy years old when he died, and he left his wife and children a fortune.

Don Martín's brand combined an E and J for Espiritu de Jesus (the spirit of Jesus). The same brand had been used by the noble de León family in Spain. It was recorded in Texas in 1807. It was the first Texas brand.

Even before Don Martín's death, Texians were beginning to resent the new laws Mexico kept passing which put more and more restrictions on the settlers. There were by then a thousand Anglos in Tejas. The newest Mexican laws said that no new immigrants were allowed to enter from the United States. Tax collectors came to Tejas from Mexico to collect taxes, which made Texians angry because they had never been taxed before. Military troops came to be sure that the new laws were followed. Texians felt that the Mexican government was interfering with their lives.

Texians wanted the government to allow more immigrants to move to Tejas. They wanted Tejas to be a separate state from Coahuila. Stephen F. Austin was the first to suggest this, as early as the late 1820s. The settlers

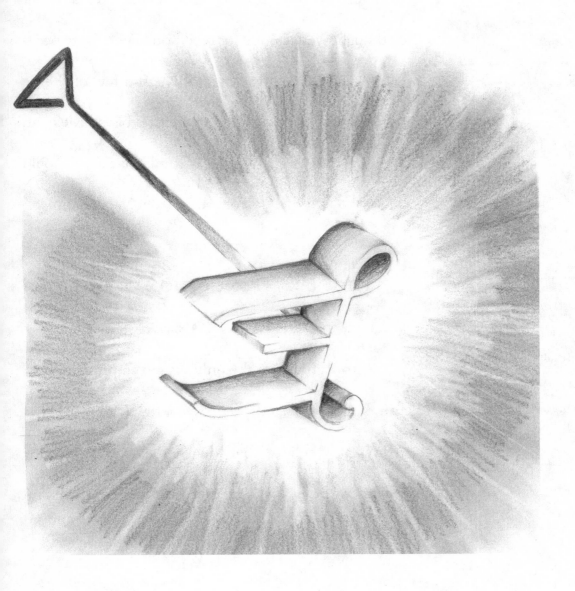

The Alamo was a mission in San Antonio. In February 1836, 189 Texians withstood a siege by about 2,000 Mexican troops under General Antonio López de Santa Anna. On March 6, the Mexican troops stormed the Alamo and massacred the Texians. "Remember the Alamo!" became a battle cry during the Texas War for Independence.

also didn't want to pay taxes. All their requests were denied, and Mexican troops began to arrest Texians that they thought were calling for rebellion. There were occasional battles, including some in which a few of the de León sons were involved. The harshness of the Mexican government made many Texians think that they should go to war to free themselves totally from Mexico.

✳✳✳

The Next Generation of the de León Family

Although he was the only Tejano empresario, Don Martín had supported the requests of the Texians. He did not, however, believe that Tejas should be completely independent from Mexico. After his death, his wife and sons continued to be closely associated with the resistance to the Mexican government of General Antonio López de Santa Anna. They agreed with their late father that Tejas should not seek total independence. They wanted more fair treatment of Texians and Tejanos by the Mexican government.

Don Fernando, the oldest son, assumed Don Martín's duties when his father died. He had received a good education, and his father had trained him in business practices. He became a respected cattleman and businessman, supervising the construction of many buildings in Guadalupe Victoria and helping to lay out the city with its public squares, church squares, and market squares. The main street of Victoria was renamed the *Calle de Los Diez Amigos* (Street of Ten Friends), honoring the ten "friends" that were the

Col. James W. Fannin and about 350 troops held the Presidio La Bahía, a mission near Goliad. When Mexican troops surrounded and captured them, the men threw themselves on the mercy of their captors. They were promised freedom, but instead were marched to a field and massacred—few escaped. "Remember Goliad!" usually followed shouts of "Remember the Alamo!"

Cholera is an infectious disease that causes diarrhea, vomiting, and cramps. People often died within twenty-four to forty-eight hours after they became sick. A person may get cholera from drinking contaminated water or eating contaminated food. When people died of cholera, their bodies were burned in pits. Then they were covered with lime to prevent further spread of the disease.

early leaders of the colony. Some of the ten friends included Don Martín, his sons Don Fernando and Silvestre, and his son-in-law Plácido Benavides. These ten men had made policies, organized defenses against the Indians, and looked out for the general welfare of the community.

Don Fernando settled on his Escondido Ranch on the Guadalupe River seven miles from Guadalupe Victoria. Escondido means "hidden." The name was appropriate because in the days of the Indian raids, many colonists hid at Don Fernando's ranch, just as they also did at his father's Santa Margarita Ranch. Years earlier, Don Fernando's wife, María, was the very first colonist to die. His only son died while away from home at college. Don Fernando later married Luz Escalera, and they adopted the two sons of his brother Silvestre, after Silvestre was killed.

Don Fernando, his brother-in-law, José M.J. Carbajal, and another colonist drove large herds of live-stock to New Orleans. Carbajal had surveyed much of the land in Victoria for the Mexican government, but he had become an active supporter of independence. The men used the money from selling the livestock to buy guns and supplies for the colonists and the Texas army. They chartered a ship, the *Anna Elizabeth*, to take them back to Texas. The Mexican government caught them, and they were put in prison. They managed to escape and return to Texas. Doña Patricia continued to work for the good of the community. She knew her sons were smug-gling arms and ammunition from New Orleans to Texas

The first shot of the Texas Revolution was fired on October 1, 1835. Colonists in Gonzales had a cannon for protection against Indian raids, and Mexican troops marched on the small town to confiscate the cannon. The townspeople fought back in what proved to be the first battle of the Texas Revolution.

Texas won its independence from Mexico at the Battle of San Jacinto on April 21, 1836. The small Texian army defeated the much larger Mexican army. General Sam Houston led the Texians.

and that it was dangerous, but she supported them in their work for Tejas.

Fernando continued to work for the cause of Tejas after his escape from prison. He was appointed an aide to acting governor James W. Robinson and was also in command of a militia unit. He had to see that the men in the unit had supplies, guns, and ammunition. He was also responsible for hiding the supplies in a safe place so that the Mexican army would not find them. When Mexican General José de Urrea occupied Victoria, he called the de Leóns traitors to Mexico and arrested Fernando and Silvestre. Urrea forced Fernando to take him to the place where they had hidden supplies for the Texian army. Don Fernando and Don Silvestre were in prison again until after the Texas victory at the

Battle of San Jacinto. They were freed because they promised to

return to Mexico, a promise they did not mean to keep.

Chapter 5

The Aftermath of Revolution and the Legacy of the de León Family

✳✳✳✳✳

After the Battle of San Jacinto many Texians resented all Mexicans. They did not see a difference between the Mexicans who had fought Texas and the Tejanos who had tried to defend Texas. They wanted to kill all Mexicans and steal their property. Newcomers took over the city of Victoria, and the de León family lost all their power. Some newcomers were honest; others were thieves.

One day Agapito, the youngest son of Don Martín and Doña Patricia, went to check on the cattle. He caught some Anglos trying to steal the family cattle. When Agapito pointed to the brand on the cattle, the gang's leader, Mabry Gray, said he had fought for Texas and therefore all that was in Texas was his. They argued with each other. Agapito was shot and killed.

General Thomas Rusk, the new general of the Texian Army, believed that Mexico would launch another attack against Texas. He began seizing Tejano property and ordering Tejanos to leave. General Rusk did not have tight control over his soldiers, and they freely stole from Tejanos and terrorized them. Once, Doña Patricia stood helpless while men stole her two donkeys, even as she begged them to leave. Don Fernando was arrested as a traitor when the Texian forces occupied Victoria. He was accused of having disclosed to Mexican authorities where Texian supplies were hidden. Having been twice arrested by the Mexican government, he was now arrested by the Texas government. His arrest did not grow out of what he had done but was a result of the growing anger of Anglos against Mexicans, even those who had

fought for their cause. While under guard he was wounded in an assassination attempt. He was finally released without a trial.

Some Tejanos fled in the face of these attacks; others fortified their ranches and swore to remain. Doña Patricia had taught her sons not to use guns against anyone. She did not want them called "bandidos." Now she had to tell them to fight back or they had to leave everything and move away. They could not go to Mexico, because they had sympathized with the Texas revolution and would not be welcome there. By the time she received General Rusk's order to leave, she had already decided to spend the summer in New Orleans. She didn't realize she'd be gone for almost ten years.

✳✳✳

EXILE!

Doña Patricia gathered the entire family, all her children and their families. They went to New Orleans, leaving behind land, furniture, money, horses, mules, cattle, and personal property worth several million dollars. The family had no money and lived very poorly in New Orleans for three years. Finally they moved to Doña Patricia's hometown of Soto la Marina in Mexico. But as Doña Patricia knew, they were not welcome in Mexico because of their sympathy to the Texas cause. Augustina de León, Don Martín and Doña Patricia's ninth child, died while the family was there. In 1840 the Republic of Texas listed the de León family among those who were behind in paying their property taxes. Texian soldiers seized their property. Don Silvestre, who had remained in Texas, was persecuted, and his property was stolen. In 1843 he made a trip to Louisiana to sell horses, mules, and cattle. On his way home he was ambushed, robbed, and murdered.

Leon County in East Texas is named for Martín de León.

Don Silvestre was an alcade. A man brought charges against Don Martín for killing his hog. Don Martín said the hog ruined his garden. Don Silvestre asked if the garden was fenced. His father said that it was, but the fence was not the best ever. Don Silvestre fined him twenty dollars, the value of the hog. He said off the bench he would still be a dutiful son but on the bench he had to enforce the law. Don Martín was proud of his son.

Some of the de Leóns returned to Victoria in 1844. Others decided to stay behind in Mexico. Doña Patricia faced a hard decision. Fernando and Felix decided to return to Texas with their families. Their mother, sisters Chucha, Francisca, and Lupita, with their families, also returned to Victoria. With some of the de León sons and daughters widowed or deceased, there were children to consider—some stayed in Mexico, and some returned to Texas.

The family returned to a city that was growing and changing. Street names were different, wooden sidewalks had been built, a fence kept animals from the market square, and Mission Indians no longer sold fruit and vegetables in the square. German farmers sold their produce. Doña Patricia found her possessions had been scattered and now belonged to newcomers in Victoria. She was no longer an important person in the town. But she resumed her work for the church. She donated the family's original homestead to the Catholic Church for a new building. Today St. Mary's Catholic Church stands on the site. Doña Patricia also donated altar vessels and a gold monstrance to the church.

Don Fernando tried to reclaim his ranch, but he only got back a portion of his original land. He had some cattle but nothing like the huge herds he had owned before the war. Many people sued him because of the goods he had been forced to turn over to the Mexican army, and he spent much of his late life fighting these lawsuits. Don Fernando displeased his mother when it became evident he, as guardian, had kept the income from the estate belonging to three of

The Evergreen Cemetery is located on the corner of N. Vine St. and W. Red River St. in Victoria, Texas. The cemetery includes grave markers for Don Martín, Doña Patricia, Fernando, Silvestre, Felix, and Agapito.

his nieces, while his mother supported them on her small income. When she died in 1850, Doña Patricia had not forgiven Fernando. He died in 1853.

Felix also went to court to regain some of his land and was successful. He and his wife Salome had seven children, the youngest born in 1847. Felix died the same year as his mother.

✳✳✳

Recognition at a Late Date

The de Leóns had no money to buy tombstones to mark the resting places of their loved ones. For one hundred years there was no monument to mark the grave of Don Martín and his family members. Finally in 1936 the state erected a gray granite marker at Victoria's Evergreen Cemetery. It reads:

Don Martín de León

Founder of Victoria. Empresario of colonial grant from

Mexico in 1824. Spanish cavalier, Indian fighter. First cattle

baron of Texas. Born in Burgos, Tamaulipas, Mexico in 1765.

Died in Victoria in 1833.

In 1972, other family members were honored with Texas state historical markers in the Evergreen Cemetery. One historian wrote that the de Leóns were "victims of the most unfair discrimination known in Texas." He went on to say that Texas had shown no gratitude for the many contributions of this loyal family. Today, finally, Martín de León and his family are recognized for their loyalty to Texas and their support of the Texas revolution. Don Martín was the only Tejano empresario and a loyal Texian, but he also passed on to his children the qualities of loyalty, honesty, and survival. He taught them the importance of family and community, and he left a legacy that speaks to the contributions of all Tejanos to Texas history.

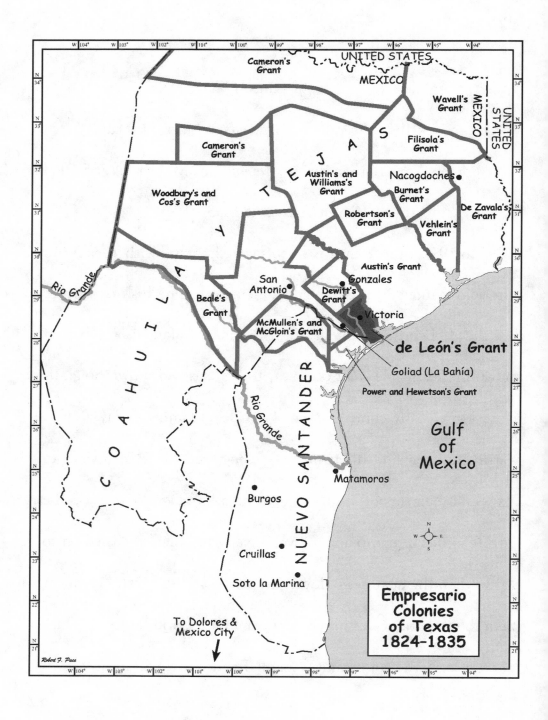

Empresario
Colonies
of Texas
1824–1835

TIMELINE

1765—Martín born in Burgos, Mexico

1785—Martín joins regiment Fieles de Burgos

1795—Martín marries Patricia de la Garza

1798—Fernando de León born in Cruillas, Mexico

1800—Candelaria de León born in Cruillas, Mexico

1801—Martín makes first trip to Tejas; returns to get family

1802—Silvestre de León born in Tejas

1804—Guadalupe de León born in Tejas

1806—Felix de León born in Tejas

1807—Martín unsuccessfully petitions Spanish governor to establish a colony near San Antonio; Martín registers EJ brand in Tejas

1808—Agapito de León born in Tejas

1810—María de Jesusa de León born in Tejas; Father Miguel Hidalgo y Costilla leads the "Cry of Dolores" uprising in Mexico; presidio troops are withdrawn from Tejas to the interior of Mexico

1812—Refugia de León born in Tejas

1814—Augustina de León born in Tejas

1818—Francisca de León born in Tejas

1823—Martín drives a large herd of livestock to New Orleans and returns on pirate ship; successfully petitions for permission to establish a colony

1824—Don Martín receives permission to settle 41 families in his colony; founds city of Victoria; founds St. Mary's Church and Nazareth Convent in Victoria

1833—Don Martín dies of cholera

1836—Texas fights for freedom; General José de Urrea arrests Fernando

1843—Sylvestre de León murdered

1849—Doña Patricia de León dies in Texas

1853—Fernando de León dies in Texas

1936—Granite monument erected for Don Martín de León

1972—De Leóns honored with Texas state historical markers in Evergreen Cemetery in Victoria

GLOSSARY

Alcalde—a mayor who also acted as a judge

Altar vessels—cups, bowls, etc. used at the altar for Holy Communion during the Mass of the Catholic Church

Ambush—to attack from a hiding place

Anglo—a white resident of the United States; not of Latin or Spanish descent

Assassination—to kill suddenly by following a plan thought out ahead of time

Ayuntamiento—Spanish for the governing council of a city

Bandito—Spanish for bandit

Cathedral—in some religions, the main church in a bishop's jurisdiction (diocese)

Discriminate—to treat another person badly because of dislike of their race or religion or some other characteristic

Dowry—the money or goods that a woman brings to her husband at the time of their marriage; the custom is not commonly practiced today

Epidemic—when a disease affects a large number of people at once

Empresario—Spanish for manager or promoter

Exile—a long separation from home or country, caused by circumstances beyond one's control

Filibuster—a soldier of fortune or an adventurer that engages in military action in a foreign country for personal gain

Jacal—a house or fence made of thin sticks driven into the ground and plastered over with mud

Karankawa—a warlike tribe of Indians found in early Texas; often thought to be cannibals

Labor (lah-BOR) **of land**—177 acres

League of land—4,428 acres

Loophole—an opening located in the walls of houses used by the occupant to fire weapons

Massacre—the wanton killing of several people

Militia—an army of citizens rather than professional soldiers

Monstrance—a container, usually of silver or gold, to hold the consecrated bread and wine for Holy Communion

Nettles—an herb covered with prickly hairs

Pack mule—a mule used for carrying goods, supplies, and freight

Petition—a formal request in writing

Persecute—to treat someone badly, unfairly

Pokeweed—a tall herb with red berries; the root was used in medicines

Presidio—a Spanish fort

Relic—something important from the past

Tejas—the Spanish word for Texas

Tejano—a Tejas resident of Spanish descent

Texian—an Anglo resident of Tejas; term used until about the 1850s

Traitor—someone who betrays his country

FURTHER READING

Alison Behnke. *Mexicans in America*. Minneapolis: Lerner books, 2004.

Debbie Levy. *Immigrants in America: The Mexican Americans*. Chicago: Lucent Books, 2003.

Frances Scarborough and H. Wedemeyer. *Stories from the History of Texas*. Whitefish, MT: Kessinger publishing, 2005.

C.J. Shane, ed. *Coming to America: The Mexicans*. Chicago: Greenhaven Press, 2005.

WEBSITES

http://www.thc.state.tx.us/publications/brochues/IndepBro.pdf (a brochure from the Texas Historical Commission that has a section on Victoria)

http://www.atlas.thc.state.tx.us/index.asp (Texas Historical Commission atlas states what is found on every state historical marker)

http://www.tamu.edu/ccbn/dewitt/deleonframe.htm

http://www.tamu.edu/ccbn/dewitt/deleon2.htm

http://www.tsha.utexas.edu/handbook/online/articles/view/DD/fde8.html

http://www.tsha.utexas.edu/handbook/online/articles/view/DD/fed81.html

http://www.tsha.utexas.edu/handbooks/online/articles/view/DD/fed80.html

http://www.tsha.utexas.edu/handbook/online/articles/view/DD/fed66.html

http://vivascancarlos.com/call_ind.html

http://www.rootseb.com/~txrefugi/DeleonMartinCensusreport.htm

http://www.texas-settlement.org/markers/victoria/21.html

http://www.tsha.utexas.edu/handbook/online/articles/DD/ued1_print.html

Index

Praise for the Stars of Texas Series:

". . . an excellent series." –*The Manhattan Mercury*

"The best way to build up a new generation of Texas history lovers is to produce books that appeal to young readers, and the good folks at State House Press are opening that door with a wonderful new series . . . 'The Stars of Texas Series' is going to be something to watch. . . . The books are fast-paced and interesting, allowing the student to quickly understand the customs and life ways of Texas history." –*Texas Illustrated Magazine*

Praise for *Henrietta King: Rancher and Philanthropist:*

". . . the kids will love the book, not realizing that it is 'good for them.'"
–*Round-up Magazine*

". . . a fine book . . . *Henrietta King* has opened the door to interest young readers to history." –*The Manhattan Mercury*

"If you want to expose your children to a truly remarkable woman, get this book."
–*Eclectic Homeschool On-line*

Praise for *Mirabeau B. Lamar: Second President of Texas:*

"Alter lets us see Lamar against the background of his era. With style and clarity, this book enables youngsters to understand a fairly complex character and his contribution to Texas history. Highly recommended for juvenile readers."
–*Review of Texas Books*

". . . the children will be so engrossed in this well-written book, . . . that the kids will never realize they are reading something 'good for them.' They will only know that they are reading a good story." –*Round-up Magazine*

"a much needed text for teaching the TEKS in Texas." –Leslie Woolsey, Region XI Educational Services Center

"*Mirabeau B. Lamar* is an excellent, youth-oriented introduction to one of early Texas' histories most important figures. This book, and others in the Stars of Texas series, offers not only excellent text, but a timeline, glossary, suggestions for further reading, websites, and an index." –*Eclectic Homeschool On-line*

Praise for *Miriam "Ma" Ferguson: First Woman Governor of Texas:*

"Recommended reading for grades 4-7: Good for research and clarity in presentation of ideas." –Carmen Antoine, Region XI Educational Service Center

"A highly valued addition to school library 'American History & Biography' collections, and 'Texas History' reading lists, *Miriam 'Ma' Ferguson* is very strongly recommended as an informative and inspiring introduction to the life and times of the Ferguson family."
–*Midwest Book Review*

"her story makes for fascinating reading. Intended for ages 9-12, this 72-page, 7x9, hardcover book offers Miriam Ferguson's tale in a highly readable format that will interest children of all ages." –*Eclectic Homeschool On-line*